Mindy Kim,
Class President

**Don't miss more fun adventures
with Mindy Kim!**

Mindy Kim,

Class President

BOOK 4

By Lyla Lee

Illustrated by Dung Ho

ALADDIN

New York London Toronto Sydney New Delhi

This book is a work of fiction. Any references to historical events, real people, or real places are used fictitiously. Other names, characters, places, and events are products of the author's imagination, and any resemblance to actual events or places or persons, living or dead, is entirely coincidental.

🪔 ALADDIN
An imprint of Simon & Schuster Children's Publishing Division
1230 Avenue of the Americas, New York, New York 10020
First Aladdin paperback edition September 2020
Text copyright © 2020 by Lyla Lee
Illustrations copyright © 2020 by Dung Ho
Also available in an Aladdin hardcover edition.
All rights reserved, including the right of reproduction in whole or in part in any form.
ALADDIN and related logo are registered trademarks of Simon & Schuster, Inc.
For information about special discounts for bulk purchases, please contact Simon & Schuster Special Sales at 1-866-506-1949 or business@simonandschuster.com.
The Simon & Schuster Speakers Bureau can bring authors to your live event. For more information or to book an event contact the Simon & Schuster Speakers Bureau at 1-866-248-3049 or visit our website at www.simonspeakers.com.
Designed by Laura Lyn DiSiena
The illustrations for this book were rendered digitally.
The text of this book was set in Haboro.
Manufactured in the United States of America 0820 OFF
2 4 6 8 10 9 7 5 3 1
Library of Congress Control Number 2020934962
ISBN 978-1-5344-4017-3 (hc)
ISBN 978-1-5344-4016-6 (pbk)
ISBN 978-1-5344-4018-0 (eBook)

To all the girls out there who
want to be president one day.
You can do it!

Chapter 1

My name is Mindy Kim. I am eight years old, and I'm now in third grade!

So far, third grade isn't as easy as second grade. There is a lot more homework, and the math is harder. But there are lots of fun new things too! We have new responsibilities, like helping our teacher, Mr. Brady, around the classroom. We also have a classroom guinea pig, Mr. Snuffles!

I sit next to Mr. Snuffles in class. He's a little smelly, but he's so cute that I don't mind. Mr. Snuffles has brown-and-white fur and large black eyes. Occasionally, he makes funny little squeaking sounds that make me smile. On special occasions, like someone's birthday, Mr. Brady puts a bow tie around his neck!

Today Mr. Brady announced that we're having class-president elections.

"I know it's October, and everyone's probably busy preparing for Halloween this weekend, but it's been two weeks since our old class president, Dill, moved away," he explained. "So we need someone to replace him. And what could be a better time to have a class election than next week, when the adults in our country will vote for a new president of the United States?"

Dill was really nice, and he was such a good class president, too! He was one of the first friends I made when I moved to Florida last year. I was really sad when he moved away.

Priscilla raised her hand. She's the girl who sits at the front of the class and always asks questions.

"Yes, Priscilla?"

"What do we have to do during the class-president election?" she asked.

"Oh, I think you were absent when we had the election last time," said Mr. Brady. "Why don't we go through the rules one more time? It's always good for everyone to have a reminder."

He smiled at all of us. "Anyone who wants to run for class president has to give a speech about why they should win. You will also need to make campaign posters and bring them to class by this Friday. You should memorize the speech if you can, so be sure to ask your mom or dad for help!"

Mr. Snuffles squeaked, as if agreeing with Mr. Brady. I wondered who Mr. Snuffles would vote for if he could!

Mr. Brady continued. "Next Monday you will give your speech, and then everyone in the class will vote for our new president. I'll pass out a fill-in-the-blank speech-planning sheet to help everyone out!"

He started handing out the sheets. When he gave me one, I stared at the paper.

We had to talk about so many different things, like our three best traits and what we would do as class president. It looked fun, but it also made me really nervous. I tucked the paper away in my backpack because just reading it made me feel scared.

When we'd first had classroom elections in August, I'd been too scared to run. I like people, but I don't like speaking in front of the class. Whenever we have to present in front of everybody for special projects, it makes my tummy hurt and I feel really dizzy.

"You should run this time, Mindy!" said Sally, my best friend. "You have so many friends. You'll win for sure!"

I shook my head. "I don't know . . . speeches are scary."

"Well, you can practice! My mom said she used to hate speeches too, but it's easy for her now since she does it almost every day for her job. You just need to practice lots and you'll be okay!"

Sally's belief in me made me all warm and fuzzy inside. Maybe she was right. Maybe I could really be the next class president!

But I was still scared. What if I froze and couldn't

5

remember a single thing? What if I talked too fast or too slow? What if my voice sounded funny and made everyone laugh?

I needed to talk to Dad. He would help me figure out what to do!

Chapter 2

Later that day, when it was time for dinner, I went into the kitchen to help Dad reheat leftovers. Yesterday Dad had made japchae, yummy Korean noodles with meat and vegetables, so we were eating that today, too.

Dad and I were both really hungry, so we watched the plate of food go around and around in the microwave. Theodore, my dog, also came over to watch!

"Dad?" I asked while we were waiting.

I opened my mouth to tell Dad about the class-president elections. But when I did, nothing came out! It was like I couldn't talk all of a sudden.

Just thinking about running for class president made my stomach feel all funny inside!

"Yes, Mindy?" Dad asked. He looked worried when I didn't say anything.

At that moment, the microwave bell went off.

"Dinner is ready!" I yelled really loudly.

Dad winced. "I can see that, Mindy. Is everything okay?"

"Yup! Totally fine. Nothing to see here! Of course!"

Dad stared at me as he put the japchae onto separate plates for the two of us. He didn't say a single thing. He just raised *one* eyebrow.

I sighed. Dad always knows what to do to get me talking.

"We're having a class-president election next week!" I blurted out. "Dill was our president, but he moved away, so we need a new one."

"Oh, that's very cool! Are you thinking of running?" Dad asked.

I hung my head and didn't say anything as I followed him to the table.

"I don't know," I said as I sat down. "I want to!

But we have to make a speech. And I hate talking in front of other people."

Dad set the plates of japchae down at the table and smiled at me.

"Well, this sounds like an excellent learning opportunity, Mindy! Best-case scenario, you'll become class president. Worst-case scenario, this will be a good chance to practice speaking in front of others. I think you should definitely try running. You'd make a great president!"

My heart beat really fast.

"Do you really think so, Appa?" I asked, calling him the Korean word for "Daddy."

"Yup! Let me know if you need my help with your speech. I'm more than happy to help out."

Dad and I started eating our food. The japchae was good, as usual, but I couldn't really focus on eating it. I was too busy thinking about my speech. Even with the guidelines Mr. Brady had given us, I had no idea what to write.

Theodore sat at my feet and looked up at me like he always does when I eat.

He was really cute, but I tried my best to ignore him. Dad says I shouldn't give him any food from the table, or else it'll become a bad habit. I went back to thinking about my speech.

"Dad, can you help me with my speech after dinner?" I asked. "Mr. Brady gave us a sheet to help us plan it out."

Dad beamed. "Of course, Mindy! We can work on it together after dinner."

After we ate dinner and washed the dishes, Dad and I sat together at the dining room table to work on the speech.

"Hmm, so, it looks like the easiest part is the beginning. All you have to do is say your name and how old you are."

"That's easy-peasy!" I said. On the piece of paper, I wrote *Mindy* in the first blank and *eight* in the second.

"Next you have to write the three things that are most important to you."

This was really easy too. "You, Theodore, and my friends!"

Dad smiled. "Good! Next you need to write three of your best traits. A trait is a word that people can use to describe you."

I thought long and hard. "Well, you always say I'm responsible. And Sally says I'm funny. But I can't think of a last one!"

"Hmm, well, you try your best to help me and your friends, so I think you're also really caring!"

I beamed. "Thanks, Dad!"

It was now time for the hardest part. At the end of our speech, we were supposed to talk about how we would help the class and why everyone should vote for us.

I gripped my pencil tightly. There were so many things I wanted to say, but there were only three blanks. I couldn't choose!

"Hmm," said Dad when I hadn't written anything for a while. "What platform do you want to run on, Mindy?"

"A platform?" I asked. "What's that?"

"A platform is like the mission for your campaign. What are some of the things you're going to

focus on and change as the class president?"

I stared down at my paper again. But no matter how hard I thought, I couldn't choose what to say.

"How about you think on it a bit more?" Dad said after a while. "I'm sure you'll think of something soon, and today's only Tuesday, so you have plenty of time. I'd be happy to look over it again when you're done!"

"Okay," I said. "Thanks, Appa!"

Even though I had no idea how to finish my speech, I still felt a lot better about everything. Writing the speech wasn't so scary with Dad's help!

Chapter 3

After thinking long and hard about my platform, I chose three things: friends, kindness, and snacks. I wanted to be everyone's friend, be nice to everyone, and give them really yummy snacks. Friendship and food are both really important parts of my life!

The next day at school, I showed my speech-planning sheet to Mr. Brady and told him I was running for class president.

"Excellent!" Mr. Brady said. "Looking forward to hearing your speech next Monday, Mindy! Remember to have the posters ready by this Friday. Oh, and wear this sticker on Monday. It's so that people know you're running for class president."

He gave me a red-white-and-blue sticker with the word VOTE! on it.

"Can I also bring snacks on Monday?" I asked. "Snacks are a really important part of my campaign!"

"Sure!" replied Mr. Brady. "Everyone can bring snacks, stickers . . . whatever you want to promote your campaign. Just be sure that your dad e-mails me ahead of time to tell me what you're bringing, in case anyone has allergies."

"Okay!"

When I showed my speech to Sally during lunch, she smiled.

"I really like your platform. Friendship, kindness, and snacks. That's so you!"

When I first moved to Florida last year, I tried to make new friends by trading my seaweed snacks with everybody at lunch. That's how I became friends with Sally!

"Thanks!" I said. "Are you running for class president?"

Sally shook her head. "Nope. But you have my vote!"

"Hey, that's not fair!" said Brandon, a boy who sits at our lunch table. "You haven't even heard her speech yet, and you're already voting for her?"

"Yeah, of course!" Sally replied. "She's my friend!"

Brandon isn't really our friend, but he still sits with us at lunch because our table is where his friends like to sit. He, Sally, and I had a big fight last year over my yummy seaweed-snack business. He's one of the meanest kids at our school.

"Are you running too, Brandon?" I asked. Mr. Brady hadn't announced who else was running, so I had no idea who I was up against.

"Yeah," Brandon said with a big, ugly grin. "That means we're rivals. I can't wait to beat you!"

"As if!" Sally exclaimed. "Mindy is way nicer than you. She's going to win!"

"We'll see about that," replied Brandon.

Suddenly I remembered what people said in movies when they were competing against each other.

I stuck my hand out. I didn't want to shake hands

with Brandon, but I had to be nice to him since I was promising to be everyone's friend as part of my platform.

"Let the best kid win," I said.

Brandon laughed and shook my hand.

"Sure. But don't cry when I beat you!"

The bell rang, and Brandon ran away, laughing.

"Jerk!" Sally called after him.

"It's okay," I said, clenching my fists in determination. "I'm going to beat him for sure."

Even though I was still scared about the speech, I wanted to win the election even more now that I knew Brandon was running too.

I couldn't let a mean kid like him become class president! Even if that meant I had to face my fears and be brave.

Chapter 4

Eunice, my babysitter, picked me up after school. Dad was working late today, so I had to stay at her house until he came back.

"Hey, how was your day, Mindy?" Eunice asked when I got into her car. "Are you excited for Halloween?"

"Yeah!" I exclaimed. "I'm also running for class president next week, so it's going to be really busy!"

It was easier to say out loud now that I was officially running. Plus, I had a really important reason to win now!

"Oh, how cool!" said Eunice. "Do you guys have

to give a speech? That's what we had to do when I was in elementary school."

"Yeah . . . ," I said. "That's the hardest part. We also have to make posters."

I looked down at my feet. Even though I wanted to win, I was still scared about the speech.

"Aw, it's okay, Mindy. I'll help you practice! How about we work on posters and go through your speech after we finish our homework? Oliver and I can be your audience."

Oliver the Maltese is Eunice's dog. He is fluffy and really cute! Theodore is the cutest dog in my book, but Oliver comes really close. Eunice and Oliver are both really nice, so practicing the speech in front of them didn't sound too scary.

"Okay!" I said.

On our way to Eunice's house, we stopped at Walmart to get supplies for posters. We bought poster paper in lots of different colors, including pink, green, white, and orange!

"I have markers and other supplies at home, so we can just use those," Eunice said.

"Wow, thanks, Unni! You're the best."

Unni is the Korean word for "older sister." Eunice isn't really my sister, but in Korean culture, I still have to call her that out of respect because she's older than me.

"No problem. Glad I can help!"

When we arrived at Eunice's house, Mrs. Park, Eunice's mom, greeted us at the door. Oliver the Maltese peeked his head out too!

"Hi, Mindy!" Mrs. Park said.

Oliver barked and wagged his tail in a really friendly way. I petted him on the head because he was a very good boy.

"Mindy has to make posters and give a speech for school," Eunice said. "She's running for class president!"

"How exciting!" replied Mrs. Park. "I still remember when you ran for class president, Eunice. You were so cute! Mindy, let me know if I can help."

"I sure will!" I said. Everyone in Eunice's family is so nice!

Homework was pretty hard. Math is my least

favorite class. Today I had a worksheet full of word problems about counting money. Word problems are really confusing, and I didn't know what some of them meant, but Eunice helped me when I got stuck.

When I finished my homework, Eunice called me out to the living room. She had the poster paper spread out on the floor.

"All right, Mindy," she said. "How about you tell me what to write and I'll help you by neatly writing your slogans on the posters? We can decorate the posters together later."

"Okay!"

We sat on the floor to make the posters. After some thinking, I came up with lots of fun slogans:

You've Got a Friend in Mindy Kim!

Vote Mindy, Vote Snacks!

Vote Mindy Kim, Everyone's Friend!

"Wow, all of these are great!" Eunice said once she was done writing them. "Now do you want to decorate them?"

"Yeah!"

I tried making the posters as cute as I could. I

drew stick figures, stars, and even flowers!

When we were done, Eunice gave me a high five. "Way to go, Mindy! These look really cute!"

"Hooray!" I cheered.

But now that we were done with the posters, it was time for the hardest part. I had to practice my speech!

Eunice helped me put the posters in a safe place and then sat on the living room couch with Oliver on her lap. Mrs. Park came over to sit on the couch too.

Everyone was staring at me!

"Okay, Mindy," Eunice said, "we're ready for you. Tell us your speech!"

My face felt really hot, like I had a fever. I was holding the speech-planning sheet, but my hands were shaking so much that I couldn't read what it said.

"H-hi," I said. My voice came out really small and quiet, like a mouse's! "My n-name is Mindy Kim."

Eunice gave me a big smile. "Maybe speak a little bit louder, Mindy!"

I glanced over at Mrs. Park and Oliver. Oliver wagged his tail at me, and Eunice's mom gave me a supportive grin.

"H-hi!" I said, trying my best to be louder. "My name is M-Mindy! I am eight years old. I . . . I . . ."

I wanted to cry. This was too scary!

"It's okay, Mindy, just try again!" Eunice said.

Oliver the Maltese wagged his tail, but even that wasn't enough for me to keep going.

I hung my head and stared at the floor. "I can't. It's too scary."

"That's all right," said Eunice. "A lot of people are bad at giving speeches. In fact, I'm pretty sure most people are at first, including me! You just have to practice, okay?"

"Okay," I said with a sigh. I was really disappointed in myself. How was I going to say the speech in front of the entire class?

"Maybe you should try saying the speech to stuffed animals first," Eunice suggested. "That's how I always practice my speeches."

"Stuffed animals?"

"Yeah!" Eunice laughed. "I still have all of mine. Even some grown-ups still have them, and that's perfectly okay! Anyway, what I like to do is put all the stuffed animals on my bed and say my speech to them. It really helps because I can make as many mistakes as I want and they'll still listen politely! Why don't you try doing that too?"

"Okay," I said.

I wasn't sure if it was going to work, but I was willing to try anything to get better at making a speech!

Chapter 5

That night, I put all my stuffed animals on my bed like Eunice suggested. A lot of them were dusty from being under the bed for so long, but I gave them all a good shake.

"Sorry, friends," I said. "Hope it wasn't too scary down there."

I put Mr. Shiba front and center, along with Mr. Toe Beans. And then I put Mrs. Poodle, Mr. Koala, and Ms. Alligator in the next row. Soon I had a whole audience waiting for my speech!

"Okay," I said. "Please be nice to me. This is my first speech!"

The stuffed animals didn't say anything, but they

still looked nice. Eunice was right. They were really polite!

I stared down at my speech-planning sheet. My hands weren't shaking like they were in Eunice's house, but my tummy still felt kind of funny.

"H-hi," I said.

I looked up from my paper. The stuffed animals were still staring at me, but they weren't scary at all. They were actually really cute!

I breathed out and tried again.

"Hi! My name is Mindy Kim. I am eight years old."

I looked up. The stuffed animals stared back. I smiled.

"I am running for class president! The things that are most important to me are my friends and my family."

Eunice was right. Practicing my speech was a lot easier with the help of my stuffed animal friends!

In no time at all, I finished my speech. It wasn't easy, but I still did it!

I tried giving my speech again. This time I was a bit better!

I was about to recite my speech a third time when Theodore came into my room. He jumped on my bed and grabbed Ms. Alligator!

"Theodore, no!"

Luckily, Theodore's legs are pretty short, so I caught him before he could run off with Ms. Alligator.

"Bad dog," I said. "Ms. Alligator isn't your toy. Give her back!"

He dropped Ms. Alligator and licked my face, so I couldn't stay mad long!

I giggled. "You're lucky you're cute."

I scooped Theodore up into a big hug.

While I was hugging Theodore, Dad popped his head into my bedroom.

"Hey, Mindy, how's that speech going? I heard you practicing. Do you feel ready to say it in front of me now?"

I gulped. Suddenly I was scared again.

"Not yet," I said. "I need to practice some more!"

"Well, all right. Just let me know, okay? I'm more than happy to listen to your speech whenever you're ready."

"Okay," I said.

Dad looked at Theodore, who was still in my arms. "Hmm, is he being distracting? Here, let me try something."

He went downstairs and came back with a brand-new bone.

"Here," he said, giving the bone to Theodore. "Hopefully, he'll be less trouble while he's chewing the bone."

I put Theodore on the floor. "Now, you be a good boy so I can practice my speech!"

Right away, Theodore sat on the floor and started chewing on the bone.

CRUNCH-CRUNCH-CRUNCH.

He looked so happy!

"Good idea, Dad!" I said. "Thanks!"

"You're welcome. Good luck with your speech!"

Dad left my room. As he was chewing the bone, Theodore stared up at me from the floor like he was one of my stuffed animals. He was now part of my audience!

I picked up my speech-planning sheet again. I

could hear the loud crunching sounds of Theodore gnawing on his bone, but the sound was so funny that it helped me feel less nervous.

"Hi, my name is Mindy Kim," I said. "I am running for class president!"

CRUNCH-CRUNCH-CRUNCH.

I laughed. Practicing my speech had just become way more fun!

Chapter 6

The next day after school, Eunice picked me up again.

"How's the speech going?" she asked when I got into her car.

"Pretty good!" I said. "Your idea worked, and I practiced a lot."

"That's great! Do you have to memorize the speech too?"

"We don't have to, but Mr. Brady said we should if we can."

Eunice sat up straighter in her seat. "You should! It looks a lot more professional if you do. It'll help you be less nervous, too! I always memorized my speeches, even when I was a little kid."

I gulped. Practicing the speech was hard enough–I didn't think I could memorize it too.

"If you're sure . . . ," I said.

"Don't worry, Mindy," Eunice replied. "You can practice with me and Oliver again!"

I still didn't know if I could do it, but I remembered what I thought about having to be brave. I had no idea if Brandon would memorize his speech, but it'd look really bad if he did and I didn't.

"Okay," I said. "Let's do it!"

Back at Eunice's house, I stood in the middle of Eunice's room while Eunice and Oliver the Maltese lay on her bed. Eunice held my speech-planning sheet in front of her as I tried to memorize it.

"Hi, my name is Mindy. I am eight years old and I am running for class president," I said. "The things . . ."

I trailed off. Giving the speech wasn't so scary anymore, but I couldn't remember what I'd said next!

"'The things that are the most important to me are . . . ,'" read Eunice.

"Right!" I said. "The things that are the most important to me are my friends and my family. I live with my dad and my dog, Theodore the Mutt! I am . . ."

I stopped again. Memorizing was really hard!

"Remember, Mindy," Eunice said. "The speech has three parts: telling the class about yourself, talking about what's important to you, and, finally, saying what you'd do to make the class better. You don't have to say what you wrote word for word, but just try to do those three things!"

I nodded and kept going.

"I am confident and love my friends. Being everybody's friend and helping others is really important to me!"

Eunice smiled. "You almost got it! I think you just need to practice a bit more and you'll be all set."

At that moment, Mrs. Park came into Eunice's room with a tray full of cookies shaped like jack-o'-lanterns.

"Happy almost Halloween!" she said. "I know

Halloween isn't until Saturday, but I wanted to make some cookies now so that you girls could bring them to school tomorrow."

"Wow, thanks, Mom!" said Eunice. She looked at me. "You've been working so hard, Mindy. You deserve a cookie break!"

"Yay!" I cheered.

"Come downstairs to eat so you don't get crumbs on the carpet," Mrs. Park said. "I also made ghost-shaped cookies!"

Eunice and I did what she said. While we were eating the cookies in the kitchen, Eunice asked me, "Do you know what you're dressing up as for Halloween yet?"

"Yup! Halloween is my favorite holiday, so Dad and I always prepare super early. We already got our costumes a few weeks ago."

Eunice laughed. "That's so cute! What are you going as?"

"A vet! That's what I want to be when I grow up. How about you?"

Eunice shook her head. "I'm too busy to go

trick-or-treating this year. I have a big exam coming up next week, so I'm just staying in and studying!"

I gasped. I felt so bad for Eunice! I'd be so sad if I couldn't celebrate Halloween.

Eunice smiled at my reaction. "It's okay. I'll hand out candy, so I still get to see fun costumes. Be sure to have *all* the fun for both you and me!"

I nodded very seriously. I was now determined to have the best Halloween ever!

Chapter 7

On Friday, the night before Halloween, I finally felt brave enough to practice my speech in front of Dad.

When I came out of my room, Dad was watching TV on the couch with Theodore. They were watching a fun action movie, but Dad turned off the TV when he saw me. I could tell he wanted to give me his full attention.

"Ready?" he asked.

I nodded. I'd said my speech so many times to my stuffed animal friends that I'd memorized everything! I hoped I would be able to say it to Dad, too.

I stood in front of the TV and let out a big breath. Dad gave me a nice, encouraging smile.

And then . . . I gave my speech! It was still pretty scary, and I had to start over three times, but on my third try I made it all the way through.

By that time Theodore was fast asleep on Dad's lap. He was so adorable that I didn't mind.

When I finished, Dad got up to clap. Theodore fell out of his lap and yelped.

"Oh no!" I yelled. "Theodore, are you okay?"

Theodore got back on his feet and wagged his tail. Dad and I laughed.

"Silly dog," I said.

I gave Theodore a belly rub. Dad came over and started scratching Theodore's head. The dog stuck out his tongue, looking really happy. He is so spoiled!

"You improved so much, Mindy!" Dad said. "I think you'll just have to practice a bit more and then you'll be all set!"

I beamed. "You really think so?"

"Yup! Keep working at it. Regardless of whether or not you get elected on Monday, I'm so proud of you for all the work you're putting into this."

"Thanks, Appa," I said.

"Hey, why don't we watch a fun movie, since tomorrow is Halloween?" Dad suggested. "I bet you could use a break."

I gasped. "Can we watch a scary movie?"

Last year Dad had said I was too young for scary movies. But I was eight now! That meant I was old enough, right?

Dad laughed nervously. "Hmm, maybe we can watch a scary movie for kids! How about *Halloweentown*?"

"Okay!"

I'd heard some kids talking about *Halloween-town* in school, but I'd never watched it myself. I was really excited!

Dad made some popcorn, and I plopped down on the couch in between Dad and Theodore. It was the perfect start to Halloween!

Chapter 8

The next morning, I jumped out of bed, all excited. It was Halloween, my favorite holiday!

"Happy Halloween!" I yelled.

Theodore barked and jumped out of bed after me. He looked really surprised.

"Sorry, boy," I said, petting him on the head. "I didn't mean to scare you!"

I changed into my vet costume, which was a doctor's white coat over pink, paw print-patterned pants. It also came with a stethoscope, and I picked up Mr. Shiba and put him under my arm as a finishing touch. I was ready for Halloween!

I went downstairs with Theodore. Dad was waiting for us in a pirate costume!

"Arr!" he said. "Shiver me theaters!"

I giggled. "It's 'timbers,' Appa."

Dad smiled. "I know. I just wanted to make you laugh!"

While we were eating breakfast, Dad checked the route to the fall carnival on his phone.

In honor of Halloween, our town was holding a big carnival, with a haunted house, a pumpkin patch, and fun rides! I was most looking forward to the haunted house, because I like scary things. I really hoped Dad would let me go into it.

We picked up Julie, Dad's girlfriend, on our way to the fall carnival. She was wearing a witch costume, and she even had a broom and a black-cat doll! She saw that I was carrying Mr. Shiba and gave me a high five.

"Great costume, Mindy! I like your dog," she said.

"Thanks! I like your cat!"

At the carnival we met up with Sally's family, the Johnsons. Sally has a big family, with two sisters and two parents! They were all dressed as super-heroes, which I thought was super cool!

Sally was dressed up as Wonder Woman. Her mom was Batgirl, and her dad was Batman! Mrs. Johnson had squarish blue glasses and looked like a grown-up version of Sally. Mr. Johnson had red hair and a nice smile. Both of Sally's parents looked really friendly. I've met Sally's mom before, but this was the first time I'd seen her dad.

Sally's parents shook hands with Dad and Julie while Sally introduced me to her sisters.

Sally pointed at her oldest sister, who was wearing a Catwoman costume.

"That's Martha. She's in ninth grade."

Martha smiled at me. She has braces, which make her look really cool. She has red hair, like Mr. Johnson.

"Hi!" I said. "Do you know Eunice? She's my babysitter, and she's in high school too!"

Martha shook her head. "There are a *lot* of Eunices at my school, but I probably don't know her. It's a big school!"

"And this is Patricia," Sally said, pointing at her other sister. "She's in sixth grade."

Patricia was dressed as Supergirl! She has blond hair like Sally.

"Hi, how's middle school?" I asked Patricia. I always heard about high school from Eunice, but I'd never really heard about middle school. It was where I was going after elementary school, so I was pretty curious.

"It's okay." Patricia shrugged. "Elementary school was more fun, though."

Once we were all done saying hi, Dad asked, "So, girls, what do you want to do first?"

"The haunted house!" I yelled, and at the same time Sally and her sisters said, "Pumpkin patch!"

Dad's face became a little green when he heard me say "haunted house." He doesn't like scary things like I do.

"Okay, we can definitely do everything at some point," he said. "But let's go to the pumpkin patch for now!"

I really wanted to go to the haunted house, but that was fine by me. The pumpkin patch was so cute! There were countless pumpkins in all sorts of shapes and sizes. Some of them were orange, while others were yellow and green. Some of them were normal pumpkins, while others were jack-o'-lanterns carved into various shapes. My favorite was the one carved to look like Snoopy!

After we were done exploring, we all gathered around for a group photo. I was so happy!

While we were walking out of the pumpkin patch, I heard people screaming in the haunted house.

"Dad!" I said. "Can we go to the haunted house now?"

Dad looked at me, and then at our group. "Hmm, I don't know. Mindy, you should ask if everyone else wants to go to the haunted house too."

"Sure, I'll go," said Martha. "I'm not scared."

"I–I'll pass," Patricia said. "I hate haunted houses."

"I want to go too!" yelled Sally. "But only if Mommy goes with me."

"Of course I'll go with you, sweetheart," Mrs. Johnson said. "I don't think you can go in without an adult anyway."

Dad sighed. "And I'll go with you, Mindy."

"Are you sure, Brian?" Julie asked. She looked a little worried about Dad. "I can go in with her if you want."

"Yeah, you don't have to if you don't want to, Dad," I said. "Mrs. Johnson will be there with me too!"

Dad shook his head. He looked really determined.

"No, it's okay," said Dad. "I'll do anything for you, Mindy. Even go into the haunted house. Let's go!"

"Yay!" I said. "Thanks, Dad!"

I was so excited to go to the haunted house!

Chapter 9

The haunted house was a big, scary-looking mansion. The sign at the front of the house said that it was an old house that used to be owned by a rich family a long, long time ago. Something bad had happened in the house, and now the house was haunted!

At the door there was a man dressed like a zombie and a lady dressed like an evil clown.

"Hi!" I said. "Can we go into the haunted house?"

The zombie and the clown stared down at Sally and me.

"Sure, kid," the zombie man said. "But only if your parents come with you."

"No problem! Come on, Dad!"

"O-okay, honey." Dad's voice sounded all weird and squeaky. I held his hand tight.

"It's okay, Dad," I said. "I'll protect you!"

Clown Lady laughed. "What a brave girl!" she said as she gave us all flashlights. "Have fun!"

We walked into the house. Sally and Martha stuck close to Mrs. Johnson, while I held Dad's hand. I wanted to keep him safe!

Inside the house it was really dark. We couldn't see anything aside from the light of our flashlights. There were strange sounds like a dripping faucet and someone laughing from very far away. Foot-steps came from behind us.

"Boo!"

A werewolf popped out of nowhere, growling and snarling!

"Ahhh!" Dad screamed. So did Sally.

"It's okay!" Mrs. Johnson said to Sally. "There's nothing to be scared of!"

I held Dad's hand tightly and yelled at the were-wolf, "I'm not afraid of you! You look like my dog, Theodore the Mutt! Go away!"

Werewolf Man looked sad as he walked away. I felt a little bad for hurting his feelings.

"Follow me," I said to our group.

As we turned the corner, a witch popped out and started cackling.

Dad and Sally screamed again, but I waved my flashlight at the witch. "Go away!"

The witch howled and ran away.

"See?" I said. "Haunted houses aren't so scary."

Mrs. Johnson laughed. "Mindy, you're one hilarious kid! Are you even shaking?"

"Nope," replied Dad. "She isn't. I'm shaking enough for the two of us."

We all laughed. Dad was so funny.

"Run away!" yelled a high-pitched voice.

A white-faced ghost snuck up on Dad and waved her arms. Dad yelped and jumped away.

"Appa, it's okay, I'll save you!"

I shined my flashlight on the ghost's face. She wailed and ran away.

"I'm so glad you're here, Mindy," Sally said. "You're braver than all of us!"

The rest of the haunted house was pretty scary, but we all made it to the exit in one piece. By the end Dad was clinging on to me very tightly. I gave him a big hug.

"It's okay, Appa. We're done!"

The workers at the exit laughed and congratulated us as we came out of the house. One of them was the werewolf from the beginning of the haunted house.

"You have a really brave daughter!" he said to Dad.

"Sorry I yelled at you, Mr. Werewolf," I said. "I was just trying to protect my dad."

The werewolf gave me a toothy grin. "It happens every time, kid–don't worry about it."

He gave me a pat on the back and handed Sally, Martha, and me ghost-shaped stickers that said I SURVIVED THE HAUNTED HOUSE!

"Yay!" I said. "I love stickers!" This was a really fun Halloween!

We met up with everyone else at the line for the Ferris wheel.

"Did y'all have fun?" Mr. Johnson asked.

"Yup!" Sally said. "Mindy protected us from everybody. She's really brave!"

"Nah, I was scared too!" I said. "But I don't think haunted houses are as scary as giving speeches."

Everyone laughed, but I was serious! I could handle witches and scary ghosts and werewolves all right, but my speech on Monday was going to be the scariest monster of them all!

Chapter 10

The day after Halloween was Sunday, the day before the class-president election. I spent all day practicing my speech and going grocery shopping with Dad. We bought snacks at the Korean supermarket so I could bring them to school on Monday.

"I checked with Mr. Brady last week, and he said no one in your class is allergic to the snacks we got today," Dad said as he tucked me into bed. "So you're all set for tomorrow!"

I pulled my blanket over my head.

"Appa, I don't think I should go to school tomorrow," I said. "My tummy feels weird."

Dad frowned and placed his hand on my

forehead. He then gave me a gentle tummy rub.

"Oh, Mindy. You're just nervous, that's all," said Dad. "It's totally okay to be scared. But just think about how brave you were at the haunted house yesterday. I'm still so amazed by what happened!"

"I just wanted to make sure you and Sally were safe," I replied. "And besides, I knew everything in the house wasn't real. Fake stuff can't hurt us. Not like real things can."

"That's true," Dad said. "Well, you were awesome at the haunted house, and I'm sure you'll be great with your speech tomorrow as well. You practiced so much!"

Thinking about my speech made the funny feeling in my belly worse. I grabbed Mr. Toe Beans, my corgi stuffed doll, and held him tightly.

"Appa, can you read me a bedtime story?"

"Sure, honey. Which story do you want me to read today?"

Dad pulled out one of my favorite books from my bookshelf. It's a collection of fun Korean folk tales that Mom and Dad bought for me the last time we visited Korea. I've already read the stories a whole bunch of times with Dad, but they're still fun!

"How about the one with the persimmon and the tiger?" I asked.

"Sure!" Dad said. He started reading me the story.

"The Tiger and the Dried Persimmon" is one of my favorite stories. It's about how a mom tricks a tiger into thinking that a dried persimmon–a yummy Korean snack–is scary, so the tiger doesn't eat her family.

"Why did the tiger think the persimmon was scary?" Even though I already knew the answer, I like how Dad always answers my question.

"Well, it's because whenever the lady mentioned the dried persimmon, her baby stopped crying. So the tiger thought that the persimmon must be *really* scary, scary enough to make babies stop crying!"

I giggled. The tiger was so silly!

Dad then read my favorite story in the entire book, "Fire Dogs." "Fire Dogs" is about the king of darkness ordering his dogs to go fetch the sun and

the moon so that the people in his kingdom can have light.

"'The sun was too hot, even for a fire dog, so the poor dogs couldn't hold on to the sun for very long,'" Dad read. "'And the moon was too cold . . . it nearly froze their mouths!' So that's the story that our ancestors told to explain why eclipses happen throughout the year. It's just the fire dogs trying to fetch!"

"Aw," I said. "I feel bad for the fire dogs. They're just trying to be good boys!"

By then I was pretty sleepy. My eyes were drooping as Dad said, "Good night, Mindy!"

He closed the door behind him, and I gave Mr. Toe Beans a big hug.

I fell asleep dreaming of tigers running away from persimmons, and fire dogs trying to grab the sun.

Chapter 11

On Monday morning I got dressed in my best presidential outfit. It was a pink button-down shirt with long black pants. I wanted to look as responsible and grown-up as I possibly could! Finally, I put the VOTE! sticker that Mr. Brady had given me on the front of my shirt. I was ready for the class-president election!

When Dad came into my room, he whistled. "Looking sharp, Mindy! Very grown-up, too."

I looked at myself in the mirror. Mom had bought the pants for me when we lived in California, and they were getting too short now. I kept growing! One of these days I'd be too big for all the clothes that Mom had bought me.

The thought made me sad, so I turned to Dad.

"I'm hungry! What's for breakfast?"

"Well, since today's a special day, I made you pancakes with chocolate chips, just the way you like them. Along with some eggs and orange juice. It's a breakfast worthy of a president for sure!"

"Hooray!" I said.

Food always makes me happy, and Dad knew just exactly what to make to cheer me up.

After breakfast, Dad drove me to school. I spotted some kids from my class who were also running for president. I could tell because they all had VOTE! stickers like I did.

Dad parked the car in the school parking lot so he could help me unload my red wagon of yummy Korean snacks. We'd bought a bunch of Choco Pie, seaweed snacks, and Pepero!

"How are you feeling about everything?" Dad asked as we went toward the school building. He pulled the wagon behind him while we walked.

"I don't know," I said. I felt better about the election than I had last week, but I still had the funny feeling in my belly.

"Well, I'll be crossing my fingers and toes for you, Mindy. Even my eyes!"

He crossed his eyes and made a silly face. I giggled. Dad is so funny.

We reached the front of the school. Dad gave me a hug before he left.

"Best of luck! Remember, no matter what happens, the most important thing is that you did your best."

"Okay, thanks, Appa."

Dad left, and I dragged my wagon of snacks through the front doors. As I went, some of my classmates turned around to point at me.

"Hey, it's the snack girl!" a kid said. His name was Peter, and he was one of Brandon's friends.

"Is she running for class president?" asked his friend Stanley.

Even though they weren't my friends, I waved hi to them on my way to Mr. Brady's class. Maybe if I was nice to them, they'd vote for me instead of Brandon!

Inside, the classroom was set up a lot differently than normal. All the desks were pushed back to make room for a podium at the front. Behind the podium were the posters of everyone running for president. All of the posters were so colorful, including mine.

The other kids also brought things like stickers, postcards, and snacks.

Sally smiled at me when she saw my wagon.

"You brought an entire wagon of snacks?" Sally asked. "That's such a great idea! Good luck! You're going to be amazing."

"Thanks, Sally! You're a good friend."

"Good morning, Mindy," said Mr. Brady. "Is that wagon of snacks for your campaign?"

"Yup!"

Mr. Brady clapped his hands together. "How creative! Please set it aside right here at the front of the classroom and go to your seat. We'll get started soon."

I did what Mr. Brady said. The first thing I saw when I sat at my seat was Mr. Snuffles. He was

wearing a red-white-and-blue bow tie. He looked so handsome!

During the morning announcements, I counted the different names on the posters. There were four other kids running besides me. One was Priscilla, the girl who always asks questions. Then there was Brandon, the mean kid. The other two were Jose and Opal, who are both really quiet and sit at the back of our class. I've only talked to Opal a few times when I've needed to borrow a piece of paper, and she is really nice!

If I didn't win, I'd be okay if anyone other than Brandon became class president.

"Okay, class," said Mr. Brady after the announcements ended. "We have five really smart and talented individuals today who want your vote for the class-president election. I'm going to need all of you to be a good audience when they're giving their speeches. Can you show them your absolute best audience behavior, just the way we practiced?"

Everyone nodded. We were all excited to hear the speeches!

"Okay, without further ado, I'll introduce you to our first candidate: Mindy Kim! Please give her a round of applause! Mindy, you're up. Step up to the podium!"

Oh no! I was first!

Everyone started clapping.

I gulped and walked around with my wagon of snacks, handing a snack to every kid before I went up to the podium.

Everyone said thanks except Brandon. He stuck his tongue out in a really mean way.

I was mad but I didn't say anything. I didn't want to make a bad impression as a presidential candidate!

When I was up at the podium, I took a deep breath and put on a brave face. I gripped both sides of the podium and set my shoulders straight, like Dad had told me to do when I was practicing.

It was time for me to give my speech!

Chapter 12

Hi," I began. "My name is Mindy Kim, and I'm running for class president! I am eight years old."

This was always the easy part, so I said it with no problem. I looked around the classroom and saw Sally quietly cheering me on.

I nodded at her and kept going. "The things that are most important to me are my friends and my family. I live with my dad and my dog, Theodore the Mutt! I am very responsible, caring, and friendly."

Out of the corner of my eye, I saw Brandon laugh and whisper something into his friend's ear. I gulped. My legs started shaking, but I kept going.

"As class president, I would make sure to be

everyone's friend. I like giving snacks, because snacks make everyone happy. And I want to make you happy too! So I will give everyone lots of snacks and make sure that everyone knows what's happening in the classroom. I'm also going to do my best to help everybody."

I was so nervous my face was hot, and my hands were really sweaty. But I was so close to being done!

"So, vote for me, Mindy Kim! Friends, kindness, and snacks for everyone!"

I bowed, and the class clapped. I was kind of dizzy, but I felt a whole lot better now that I was done.

When I sat down in my seat, Sally patted me on the back.

"You were great!" she said. "I'd vote for you even if you weren't my friend!"

"Thanks, Sally!" I said.

"Great job, Mindy!" said Mr. Brady. "It's not easy going first, but you did an amazing job. Next up is Brandon Paulson. Brandon, come on up!"

A lot of the boys in our class cheered.

Brandon pumped up a fist into the air and said, "Yes! Finally it's my turn!"

Brandon was really good at speaking, and he didn't look nervous at all. The more he spoke, the more his friends cheered. By the time he was finished, I was sad. It looked like he was going to win for sure.

"Don't give up!" Sally said. "You never know who'll win!"

I nodded. She was right.

The other three kids were really good too. I especially liked Priscilla's speech, because she said she would help make our classroom be the very best it could ever be. Her poster had a picture of Mr. Snuffles on it, which I thought was really funny!

And then, finally, it was time to vote. Everyone wrote down their pick on a piece of paper and dropped it in the ballot box at the front of the room.

"I'll announce the winners at the end of the school day," said Mr. Brady. "But for now, it's time for lunch!"

Lunch went by super slowly, and so did the rest of the school day. I ate and worked and played at recess like I normally did, but my mind was on the class-president election. I really wanted to win!

When it was time for the class-president announcement, Mr. Brady stood at the front of the class with a small piece of paper. The paper with the name of the winner!

"Okay, class," Mr. Brady said. "Thank you for being patient. Everyone was so great. I've counted up the votes and will now announce the name of the class president. Everyone did such a good job, and I'm proud of everyone who ran. It was a close race!"

Finally it was the moment of truth!

Chapter 13

"Everyone should be proud of themselves, including the people who didn't run, but voted," Mr. Brady continued. "You all made your vote count, just like your parents will hopefully do on Election Day tomorrow!"

"Just tell me I won already!" yelled Brandon.

Mr. Brady frowned. "Brandon, please calm down. Friends, what do we do when we want to talk?"

Everyone raised their hands.

"Yes, Priscilla?"

"We raise our hands!"

"Very good!"

Brandon grumbled and slumped into his seat. He was not being a good candidate!

"He's such a big baby!" said Sally. "I really hope he doesn't win."

Mr. Brady waited until we all quieted down before clearing his throat.

"Okay, class. The next president of Room 303 of Wishbone Elementary for the 2020-2021 school year is . . ."

I held my breath and crossed my fingers and toes. I closed my eyes, too. I really hoped I would win!

"Priscilla Jones!"

Everyone cheered and clapped. I opened my eyes. I was sad that I didn't win, but I was really glad that it wasn't Brandon.

"Yay, Priscilla!" I said, joining the people cheering for her. Opal and Jose said yay too. We were all happy for her!

Priscilla is always the one who asks all the questions and makes sure she understands everything. She is really smart and nice, too! I hoped she would make our class great.

The only person who wasn't cheering was Brandon. He looked really mad, and his face was red.

"No fair!" Brandon shouted. "There needs to be a recount. I deserved to win!"

"Brandon!" said Mr. Brady. "I am very disappointed in you. Please sit with me in the classroom during recess tomorrow."

I cheered on the inside. Even though I hadn't won the class-president election, I was still happy.

After school, Dad came to pick me up. Eunice usually picks me up, so I was surprised!

"I wanted to see how my presidential candidate did on her big day," Dad explained. "Luckily, I'm between projects right now, so I could leave work early! How did the election go?"

"I didn't win," I said.

"Aw, I'm so sorry, Mindy," replied Dad.

"It's okay. Priscilla Jones won, and she's really nice and smart. I'm glad she won!"

Theodore was in the car with us. He licked my face, like he wanted to cheer me up.

"Tell you what," Dad said. "Even though you didn't win, I think you still deserve a prize for working so hard on your speech. You improved so much, and that's a really big accomplishment! Why don't we go get milkshakes on our way home?"

"Yay!" I yelled.

I love milkshakes! And I love spending time with Dad.

"You know, Mindy, I was just thinking," Dad said on our way to the milkshake shop. "The things that you promised in your speech—being everyone's friend, being nice to everybody, and giving out snacks— those are all things that you can do on a day-to-day basis. You don't have to be the class president to do all three! So even though Priscilla is the class president, why don't you try to help people and set a good example for everyone else in the class too?"

"Okay, that's a great idea!"

As we sipped our mint-chocolate milkshakes, I knew Dad was right. And even though I hadn't won, I was still really happy. I'd made a really good speech! I hadn't forgotten my words! And someone really great was our class president.

Today was a good day.

Chapter 14

Priscilla is a really good president, just like I thought she'd be. She leads the class during the Pledge of Allegiance, is really fair when assigning classroom jobs, and does her best to help everyone too! Even though I'm still kind of sad that I didn't win, I'm glad that the job went to the perfect person.

A week later there was a new kid in our class. Mr. Brady said her name was Lindsey and that she'd just moved here from Minnesota. She looked really shy. She didn't know anyone and didn't have any friends yet, just like I hadn't when I was the new kid last year, in second grade.

During lunch, Lindsey sat alone. She looked really sad! I remembered what Dad had told me, and I decided to try to help.

"Hey!" I waved at her.

She pointed at herself, like she couldn't believe I was talking to her.

"Me?" she asked. Her voice sounded quiet and scared.

"Do you want to sit with me and my friend Sally?" I asked. "You can try some of my snacks!"

Lindsey's eyes widened, but then she slowly smiled.

"Okay!" she said.

Lindsey sat at our table. She didn't say anything at first. But Sally and I asked her questions to get her talking.

"What's your favorite color?" Sally wanted to know.

"And what's your favorite animal?" I asked.

"I really like blue," she said. "And I love horses! I used to have a pony at my old house. I miss her so much. Her name is Betsy!"

Lindsey showed us a picture of her pony. It was a brown pony with really cute eyes!

"Wow, you had a pony?" Sally asked. "That's so cool!"

"Sorry you don't have her anymore, though," I said.

"Oh, it's okay. She's with my grandparents now. We're going to visit them back in Minnesota on Thanksgiving!"

"That's good," I replied. "Sally and I both love dogs. I have a puppy named Theodore the Mutt!"

By the end of lunch, Sally, Lindsey, and I had talked a lot about everything and anything. We were all friends now!

Even though I hadn't won the election, I was really glad I could help Lindsey. Being the class president is important, but so is being a good friend and being kind to other people. And I was so happy that I now had a new friend!

It looked like my platform of friends, kindness, and snacks had worked after all.

Acknowledgments

First and foremost, I would like to thank *you*, Reader. Thank you for reading this book, and the previous Mindy Kim books, if you've read them. Thank you especially to those of you who've told me (either directly or through an adult) how you enjoyed reading about Mindy's adventures. The year 2020 was my first year as a published author, and it hasn't always been easy, but what makes everything worth it is hearing from readers like you. Keep reading! There are so many different worlds and stories out there. I hope you never lose your love of books.

Next, I'd like to thank my parents, who supported me when *I* ran for class president in elementary school. Thank you also for listening to my class presentations, choir recital practices, and whatever else I needed help with when I was in school. Even though you weren't always able to help me with what I learned in school and didn't always understand English, I still appreciate how you did your best to help me through everything.

I'd like to also thank my friends, as always. Whether you're in Asia, Europe, Australia, or elsewhere in North America, I am so grateful for all of you. Thank you for being there for however long we were and/or are friends. Just like Mindy is lucky to have a friend like Sally, I am so fortunate to have friends like you.

To all the teachers, booksellers, parents, and librarians who encourage kids to read every day: thank you. I am the writer I am today because of the teachers, booksellers, librarians, et cetera, I met while growing up, so I know you're having an equally big impact on these children's lives. And to the parents who do their best for their children like my parents did for me: you're all rock stars. You inspire me daily with what you do, especially in the bumpy and uncertain year we've had.

Finally, I would like to thank everyone who is involved in the process of making the Mindy Kim books into a reality. Never in my wildest dreams could I have imagined having a children's book series of my own, and yet here we are now, releasing a fourth book of this series. What a wild and exciting journey it's been! Thank you for helping make my childhood dream into a reality. Fourth-grader Lyla would be so happy to know that dreams come true after all.

About the Author

Lyla Lee is the author of the Mindy Kim series as well as the YA novel *I'll Be the One*. Although she was born in a small town in South Korea, she's since then lived in various parts of the United States, including California, Florida, and Texas. Inspired by her English teacher, she started writing her own stories in fourth grade and finished her first novel at the age of fourteen. After working various jobs in Hollywood and studying psychology and cinematic arts at the University of Southern California, she now lives in Dallas, Texas. When she is not writing, she is teaching kids, petting cute dogs, and searching for the perfect bowl of shaved ice. You can visit her online at lylaleebooks.com.

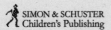